DOORS INTO CHANCE

Stories from Archers Beach

Sharon Lee

Copyright Page

"The Road to Pomona's," Splinter Universe (www.splinteruniverse.com) 2016; collected in *Horror for the Throne,* Fantastic Books, August 2021

"The Vestals of Midnight" *Release the Virgins*, edited by Michael A. Ventrella, Gray Rabbit Productions, January 2019

"Wolf in the Wind" first incomplete publication on Splinter Universe (www.splinteruniverse.com), September 2023

Introduction to "Wolf in the Wind" partial appeared on Splinter Universe (www.splinteruniverse.com), August 2023

Author's Note is original to this chapbook

ISBN: 978-1-948465-24-3

Cover art: SelfPubBookCovers.com/RLSather

Published February 20, 2024 by Pinbeam Books

Pinbeam Books

PO Box 1586

Waterville ME 04903

email info@pinbeambooks.com

Thanks to Intrepid Tyop Hunters

Kirsten Guyaz, Marni Rachmiel, and Kate Reynolds.
Any remaining infelicities in the text are absolutely the fault of the author.

Table of Contents

The Road to Pomona's

"*Elinor*." He sighed; she was off *again*. You'd think she didn't want—

"Hmm? Did you say something, Charles?"

"Did I say—Elinor, we are trying here to plan our vacation—something I think we *both* want very much?" It was lost on her. She only looked at him, face composed, eyes empty of any hint of emotion. Of involvement.

He tried a different tack, pushing the papers and travel brochures together into a hasty pile and stacking them atop the refrigerator, theoretically out of the cat's territory.

"Listen, I'm beat, myself. Tomorrow's Saturday, we'll have the whole day to just mess around and talk about plans. It was stupid to try it tonight, anyway. Let's go to—"

Amazement stopped him. Elinor was sitting stiffly upright, face, for once, intent. "What did you say?"

"What did I—when?" He was honestly baffled.

"You said tomorrow's Saturday. *Saturday*. It can't possibly be Saturday . . . "

"It can't?" Charles stared. "Why can't it? I've waited a whole—"

Again, her face interrupted him. "OK, suppose *you* tell *me* what day tomorrow is."

She looked a little bewildered herself. "Well, all right—Saturday. I guess. It's just that I promised Pomona—"

"Pomona? Who's Pomona? And why'd you promise her anything? You knew perfectly well that this is the first Saturday I've had off in—HEY!"

But Elinor was already gone, racing down the short hallway to their bedroom.

1

* * *

The road to Pomona's is tree-lined and dim. You move for a timeless time over white gravel, the breeze that cools your face scented with roses and lilac. Suddenly, you stand out upon the hillside and there it is, set like a jewel in the very heart of the valley, an island of serenity in a sea of deep red grass ...

* * *

"Elinor? Elinor, why're you sitting in the dark?"

She stirred, focused. "I've got a headache. The light bothers me."

"Oh." He moved into the room, sat on the corner of the bed. She could just see him, a dim, slumped-forward outline, hands clenched between his knees.

"Listen, Elinor . . . ." He paused.

"I'm listening, Charles."

"I—well, *look*, if you don't want the vacation, or you want to go someplace else—I mean, you should *say* so, right? It's not like we have to—I just thought—hell, all the overtime I've been doing, we ought to get something out of it. But if you'd rather not . . . "

"Oh, no. No, Charles, Las Vegas sounds *lovely*—" she suppressed the mental image of hot, bright lights; too many bodies; too much noise. "I think we'll have *lots* of fun. Really I do."

The outline of his shoulders straightened in the dimness. "That's the truth, now?"

"Cross my heart." She moved to sit beside him; rested her forehead against his arm. "I warned you, didn't I? I'm impossible. I *told* you so—moody, irascible. But, no, nothing would do but that you marry the wench—" She pounded him lightly on the back with one half-serious fist. "I *warned* you, you bully—"

He laughed; swung an arm around to pull her close. "OK, you did. The blame's on me. Sometimes, it's almost worth it ..."

Much later, at the very edge of dreaming, he remembered.

"Elinor. Who's Pomona?"

He was already asleep when she answered, "Oh, nobody—really."

She woke before him next morning; snuck away for a quick shower; pulled on jeans and a bright red sweater and went down the hall to the kitchen, running fingers through still-damp hair.

The cat was fed first, as always, she murmuring breakfast pleasantries; he aloof, but polite. She clicked on the radio, pushed open the window above the sink and turned back, hands on hips, to frown around the kitchen. "Pancakes, I think?" and then grinned. "Why not? Saturday comes but once a week—"

Eggs, milk, and sausage were out of refrigerator like a conjuring trick; the skillet was set to heat and the coffeepot primed. She sang with the radio as she worked. The breeze came through the window, carrying the scent of fresh-mown grass from the park across the street.

* * *

The road to Pomona's is tree-lined and dim. You move for a timeless time over white gravel, the breeze that cools your face scented with roses and lilac. Suddenly, you stand out upon the hillside and there it is, set like a jewel in the very heart of the valley; an island of serenity in a seat of deep red grass. And within, Pomona herself, whose house is but a reflection of her own deep and healing peace. She busies herself, perhaps, at her spinning, or makes music upon a crystalline keyboard. Though, again, perhaps not today. For tonight there is to be celebration in Pomona's house, and there are preparations to be made. Best you not tarry, then, upon the hill; for here is one place where actuality surpasses anticipation.

"Morning, Spike!" She felt herself whirled about, mechanically returned an exuberant kiss. "Pancakes, huh? Super! *Real* coffee? Time for a fast shower? I'll be right back—save some for me, now!"

She was humming with the radio again by the time he returned.

They ate, Charles putting pancakes into his mouth at an alarming rate and, at the same time, chattering about the proposed trip to Vegas. Elinor pushed bits of soggy pancake and sausage around her plate, remembering to glance up every now and then, and smile.

He ran down, finally, and leaned back in his chair, third cup of coffee held reverently in his hands, and grinned at her. "My dear, you have outdone yourself. If this is what I miss by working on Saturday—"

The road to Pomona's is tree-lined and dim—

She was jerked to her feet, "—to the zoo!" Charles was laughing.

"The zoo?" The shock of transition made her stupid.

"Sure, the zoo. It's bright sunshine; we should take advantage." He leaned forward conspiratorially, "I'll buy you an ice cream." Then he was charging to the front door, Elinor in tow.

"The dishes!" she cried.

"Let the cat do 'em!"

And they raced down the apartment-house stairs and into the street, laughing identical laughter.

* * *

The road to Pomona's is tree-lined and dim. You walk for a timeless time over white gravel, the breeze that cools your face scented with roses and lilac. Suddenly, you stand out upon the hillside and there it is, set like a jewel in the very heart of the valley; an island of serenity in a sea of deep red grass. Dusk is approaching now and already candles are being lit in the windows to show the way to those few who do not know it by heart. A festival tonight, the candlelight murmurs across the valley; a celebration for our true friend, our Elinor. Come, come all, to meet Elinor; to welcome Elinor . . .

". . . Elinor. Come to bed." He sat next to her on the loveseat, reached out uncertainly. "Hey, are you all right? I mean, can I get you anything or something?" His hand smoothed her short, rough hair. "Spike? You there?"

She focused slowly, read the concern in his face, made the effort: "Too much excitement today, I guess. I'm not used to doing much on Saturdays, since you've been working. I'm a little—keyed up."

He looked relieved. "Keyed up, eh? Well, ol' Doc Charles has a cure for *that*, little lady. Just you stay right here one minute while I mix it up."

He vanished, and she heard him rummaging in the kitchen. His minute stretched into five while she carefully noted the signs of wear in the carpet; the pattern of the traffic light on the shade.

It *had* to be tonight—the Gate would only admit her fully tonight. Elinor closed her eyes, hearing Pomona's voice explaining it, over the *sshussh* of her spinning: "It will not be difficult. You already know the way . . . To the ones you leave on the other side—it will only look to them as if you had died."

Charles thrust a warm mug into her hand. "Down the hatch."

She swallowed obediently. Warm milk and brandy.

"All of it."

She showed him the empty mug. He took it back to the kitchen, reappeared and pulled her to her feet.

"Now to bed." A finger across her lips stifled a fledgling protest. "Don't argue with your doctor, girl; he knows best. Woman your age needs her sleep. So, c'mon; let's tuck you in."

After he had turned off the light and settled in his side of the bed, she murmured, "Charles?"

"Hmm?"

"I love you, Charles."

"I love you, too, Spike. G'night."

"Good-bye."

* * *

The road to Pomona's . . .

The Vestals of Midnight

You've been there, right? The moment when you're startled out of a sound sleep because someone is walking on your land who doesn't belong there?

Who *seriously* doesn't belong there?

Curled on my side, eyes closed, snugged into blankets still warm from Borgan's presence, I reached for the Land . . .

It was early—or late, depending on your inclination and service. Borgan'd left ten minutes ago, to go out for the day's fishing. Those who prospered in the dark were thinking about pulling themselves into their places for a snooze, while those who had no cause to hide from the sun's face were drifting toward wakefulness. . .

There.

I snatched at the shiver of wrongness; pushed the Land to *show me*; and sat up straight in bed.

There?

Who in God's name would try to sneak up on the Enterprise?

I mean, the Enterprise *is* on my Land – by which I mean, it's in Archers Beach, of which I am, for a bunch of complicated reasons, mostly having to do with sin, and bloodlines, and—I'm sorry—magic, the Guardian. Geography being what it is, the Enterprise is in my—call it *my jurisdiction*. In theory, this means it's also under my authority.

Feel free to tell that to the Enterprise. I'll wait.

Still keeping a tight fix on that sliver of wrongness on the Land, I opened my mundane eyes to my bedroom. Breccia the cat was sitting up tall at the bottom of the bed, ridiculous floof of a tail wrapped primly around her toes; her eyes serious. Outside, I could hear the

7

ocean playing with the shore; the view out the window was grey sea-mist against dawn-grey sky.

The imminent rising of the sun was causing the stranger on my Land some concern, and they weren't making any particular effort to hide that worry—or themselves.

Which in turn worried *me*.

I threw back the covers, pulled on jeans, sweater, socks, sneakers; nodded to Breccia.

"Hold the fort," I told her. "Be right back."

Then I reached to the Land again, and stepped from my bedroom . . .

Into the dooryard of the Enterprise, which was shrouded in something much denser and more malevolent than mere fog; heavy with a despair that reminded me forcibly of a Black Dog.

There was magic building. Specific, sophisticated, magic, and the Enterprise was its intended target. I drew on my own power, and looked closer, seeing the sticky ball of compulsion and command revolving in the thick air; saw, more importantly, the dark figure at the heart of the darkness, cloak billowing in a breeze I didn't feel; the spell very nearly complete, spinning between the palms of their hands, spitting sticky black sparks of malice.

I took a deep breath, drew a tad more power, and spoke.

"That," I said, conversationally, "would be a bad mistake."

The Land boomed; the air crackled. The dark figure jumped, the bomb they'd created snapping out of existence with a pettish little *fsst*, like a wet firecracker.

A breeze rushed through the clearing, chilly and tasting of salt. The unnatural fog shredded, and I was facing a stocky woman wearing a long black gown under the black cloak, bodice laced with blood-red ribbons, sleeves dripping with crimson lace. Her face was pale and round, and she was wearing sunglasses.

"How dare you interfere with me?" she snapped.

"In the job description," I said. "I'm the Guardian of Archers Beach, and you were about to do something really stupid, which, just as a side effect, could've killed us all."

I paused, and added, in case it wasn't clear.

"*You* would have been included in *us all*."

She took a breath that strained the bright ribbons.

"That . . . entity," she said, moving a hand glittering with dark gemstones toward the Enterprise, "has stolen from me."

A word here about the Enterprise. In these parts—these parts being the state of Maine, on the East Coast of the United States—an "enterprise" is a kind of a cross between a junkyard and a flea market. You can find all kinds of *stuff* at an enterprise, from silver teapots to Nixon/Agnew campaign buttons; from slate chalkboards to yellowed lace doilies, to bags of mismatched Legos®.

The Enterprise in Archers Beach also deals in *stuff*: magical stuff, hexed stuff, stuff nobody heard of, stuff nobody wants, and stuff somebody might want 'way too much.

The assertion that the Enterprise had *stolen* from this nice lady didn't particularly shock me. I'd long wondered where the the Enterprise's *stuff* came from. Artie, the *trenvay* whose duty the Enterprise was, could only tell me that "things come in," from time to time, on their own schedule, and with their own ideas. He didn't know where they came from, or necessarily how they arrived. They appeared, was all. Artie's part of the business was to make certain that those things which came in with a purpose or a name attached were delivered to their proper recipients, and the rest were kept—quiet.

But that's getting ahead of things, just a little. There were courtesies to be observed between visitor and Guardian. She should have offered first, being a stranger on my Land, but I could afford to be gracious.

On my Land.

So I bowed, and said easily.

"I'm Kate Archer, Guardian of the Land; heir to Aeronymous, late of the Land of the Flowers."

I got the impression that I'd startled her; that maybe she'd blinked behind those dark glasses. If so, she recovered fast, and produced a very nice bow, indeed.

"I am Annora of Shadowood, in service to the Queen of Daknowyth."

Daknowyth. The Land of Midnight, that would be. Not quite my favorite of the Six Worlds, but it did explain the sunglasses and the concern about the coming dawn.

"So, what exactly did the Enterprise steal from you, and how would blowing it up get whatever it is back?"

Annora bristled.

"I am on the business of my Queen!" she snapped.

"You're on the business of your Queen *on my Land*," I countered. "Since the business of your Queen seems to include *blowing things up* on my Land, I'd—"

"If you had bothered to understand what I was doing," she interrupted sharply; "you would have seen that my intention was to smother everything magic-touched in this area. My . . . items, which are not so touched, would then have been easy to remove."

"That might have been your intention," I said. Admittedly, I'm not very good at spell-craft; for all I knew, her sticky bomb really *had been* only a fire-blanket. But smothering the Enterprise wasn't any better, in the long run, than blowing it sky-high. Worse, really. The Enterprise is used to getting its way.

"Still not a great idea to interfere with the Enterprise."

"Am I to reason with it?" Annora inquired, with a certain amount of justifiable sarcasm.

"No," I said, giving her the point; "that never works. We'll have to reason with the *trenvay*—the spirit of the place—involved . . . ." Which *some*times worked.

"Now, how about—"

"Kate?"

The door to the Enterprise opened, spilling yellow light into the dooryard. Annora hissed and moved a hand; the light dimmed perceptively as the shadow that was Artie came forward.

"Kate," he said again, ignoring Annora entirely.

"We got a problem."

"I should say *so*!" Annora snapped, and took a deep breath, like she'd remembered where she was, and continued more moderately. "You can cease to have a problem. Merely release them to me."

Artie turned his head, and considered her for a length of time just shy of insulting before turning back to me.

"Who's this?"

"This," I told him, "is Annora of Shadowood, on the business of the Queen of Daknowyth."

"Daknowyth," Artie repeated, like you might say *jellyfish*. He turned back to me.

"What's the trouble?" I asked, to forestall a long detour about Daknowyth, its Queen, and its history, or lack of same, with our very own Changing Land.

"Well," he said, rubbing the back of his neck in a fair semblance of bewilderment. "We got something come in, all right—couple of somethings, if it come to that—but it ain't—*they* ain't—in the usual way."

He paused, and looked me straight in the eye, which was when I knew—*really knew*— just how worried he was.

"An' if we don't get 'em outta there soon, there's no telling what'll happen."

#

The Enterprise is one smallish three-room shed, and the yard behind it. Every square inch is covered in stuff, and sometimes there's stuff inside the stuff.

Mundane folk—by which I mean people who are magic-blind—mundane folk are the Enterprise's fair game. All summer long, ordinary people walk into the Enterprise, meaning only to stay a couple minutes, ducking in out of the sun, maybe, or just mildly curious. Certainly, they never mean to *buy* anything.

And yet, all summer long, those folks go home with this or that little souvenir that, when questioned, they have only the haziest recollection of having purchased; an ugly little thing, but for some reason, they just can't seem to bring themselves to get rid of it. No one would suggest that there was anything . . . magical . . . in that. Magic wasn't real, after all, and for most of the people in the world—it's just not there. They don't *feel* the energy sparking all around them; they don't *hear* the strange music intended to pull them into a dance they can't hope to survive; they don't *see* the beautiful woman beckoning to them from the wood, and they *certainly* don't follow her off the path.

Magic folk—like me, like Annora of Shadowood, like Artie—magic folk have their own defenses and strategies to answer the lure of the Enterprise. That's not to say that we're not occasionally caught unaware, but the mischief made with us tends to be minor.

No, it's half-magic folk—those who *can* see the weird, but who have no magic of their own—who're in the most danger from the Enterprise—and the risk to them is utterly non-trivial. In most cases, it's life-changing. And not in a good way.

In the old days, they were locked up in attic rooms, or insane asylums. In these enlightened times, we've got drugs for that. The weakest can't prevent magic seeping into them, filling them up until they're no longer, really, themselves.

The strongest make it a policy never to walk down dark alleys, speak to strangers, or to look too nearly into the shadows cast by the street-lights. I don't imagine that they ever sleep sound, but I believe most of them survive.

"The light is increasing," Annora said voice calm, though the Land brought me the sharp stab of her concern.

I sighed.

"Right. Let's get this thing done."

#

There were no mundane customers in the Enterprise this early in the day. That might've been the reason for the extra fizz in the air. Magical being that I am, and Guardian of the Land, too, I could still feel the aisles crowding me, and something a lot like something big, hungry, and with lots of teeth breathing down the back of my neck. The air was alive with whisperings; no words that the ear could actually catch, mind, but you were left with the idea that the Enterprise found you, just faintly, ridiculous.

"What is this place?" Annora asked from behind me. "Why has it not been tamed?"

Behind us, to the left, something . . . growled.

"A little tact might be in order," I said, when the growl had subsided into whispers again.

"Enterprise is old," said Artie, who was bringing up the rear. "Older'n me, and I'm plenty too old. Back when Kate's grandma was a saplin', we got to talking about it one day with the Ol' Forest. Best we could figure, then, was the Enterprise is more gate than anything else, an' most of it's Out Beyond, blowing in the Wind Between the Worlds. Figured that was how stuff come in like it does. I never figured any better. Ain't like it talks to me, really."

"Surely, it will amend itself out of respect for the Guardian," Annora said.

I didn't laugh, but the Enterprise did, lights flickering, and wooden floorboards groaning.

"So, Artie," I said over my shoulder. "Where are these things that just came—"

I stopped, because here they were, of course, and their danger was horrifyingly real.

They were in the second, middle, room of three, as surrounded by the Enterprise as it was possible to be. The room was slightly lower than the first room—three steps down from the floor I stood on, to the floor they stood on, pressed in on all sides by rustic bureaus, spinning wheels, three-legged stools, rocking chairs, and an unstrung harp.

Six youngers, ranging in age from maybe-eight to maybe-twelve, stood in two rows, facing the far wall, the three tallest in front. They were wearing dress native to each of the Six Worlds. Black gown and cloak for the dark Daknowyth miss with the white-as-opal

eyes; sky-blue tunic for the pale winged one from Varoth; crimson
and black for the fiery redhead from Kashnerot; waterskins, high
boots, and a demi-cloak for the haughty dark-haired youth from
Cheobaug; bright silks and a crown of sweet flowers on the head of
the child from Sempeki; jeans so old they were white, tennis shoes,
and a black t-shirt with a band logo faded 'til I couldn't read it, from
our own, the Changing Land.

"*Kids?*" I snapped, and turned to Annora, flinging out a hand in
an *explain this* gesture.

"Vestals," she corrected. "Each has accepted the Word of the
Queen of Daknowyth and bound themselves to her honor."

"Do their parents know?" I asked.

"In every case, they are kinless," Annora told me with dignity.
"The Queen of Daknowyth is not a thief."

"Kate . . ." Artie said from behind me, and I could hear the strain
in his voice. "They can't stay here much longer, and I mean *much*.
They're all of 'em empty!"

Turning back, I saw what he meant.

The room was dim; expectable, given the hour and the fact that
the Enterprise was poorly lit by design.

The kids, though—the kids were standing in a spotlight of pearly
light, each casting a shadow of lambent silver. I realized then that I
was looking at innocence; at purity, if you'll allow it. None of them
possessed the least shred of magic. All of them could see the weird;
taste it; hear it. Their one defense was their virtue—and that wasn't
going to be enough.

Magic, in case I forgot to say earlier, abhors a vacuum. It will
strive to fill any empty vessel with itself. The Enterprise, being old in
guile and in magic, desired nothing more than to fill each of those
kids up with itself, and possess them, utterly.

The Land trembled with the Enterprise's lust, and I started to feel a little sick. No time for that now. *Now*, I looked deeper, and—yes; there were dark flares and flashes just beyond that nimbus of purity, chewing away at the edges, but not, I noticed, too quickly. The Enterprise was enjoying this game, and had a mind to stretch it out.

"That will do!" Annora stepped forward, and I dropped back a step to let her have a full view of the situation.

"These are not yours to take!" she cried, power thrumming in her voice. "These are the Vestals of Midnight. They are under the shield of the Queen of Daknowyth, which I, her appointed representative, now extend!"

That quick, something black, supple and complex flowed out and over the room, drifting like a sweet cloud over the heads of the six kids. It was, I saw, intended to envelope them, like armor, whereupon, they could be led out of center of the Enterprise's ravenous web.

Except, it never settled.

The . . . things that had been gnawing at the edge of the circle of light abruptly merged into a blare of oily lightning, stabbing straight into the heart of the cloud.

Thunder boomed. Sparks flew. The furniture lunged forward, legs clattering like hooves on the old wooden floor.

The red-haired boy yelled and thrust out a hand, catching a flying sugar bowl nd throwing it at a book that was flapping toward them like a raven.

The kid from the Changing Land kicked out, in perfect form, smacking a charging spinning wheel with the flat of her sneaker, sending it crashing back into a bookcase filled with ugly knick-knacks.

"Hey!" Artie yelled. "You be careful! Them things is worth money!"

In the doorway, Annora gestured. I felt power surge, saw a second iteration of the black shield flow into being—only to be torn to shreds by the Enterprise's outrage.

It was only a matter of seconds before things started breaking, and there was no assurance that the kids would survive the battle of wills.

On the other hand, Annora *was* drawing the Enterprise's fire.

I reached to the Land, and through it spoke directly to the kids.

"Let's go! Run! This way!"

They tried. The girl from the Changing Land and the boy from the Land of Wave and Water each grabbed the hands of the two kids nearest them and dragged them forward. The first three steps were fine—not a run, but brisk enough—the fourth step was like they were walking through mud; the fifth step—well, the Changing Land kid managed a fifth step, but none of the rest of them did.

The Enterprise *roared*!

Dust blew up in swirling plume, crockery broke, a stool danced a tango across the floor, slammed into a rocking chair, and knocked it onto its back.

Annora groaned. I could see her struggling to raise yet another wave of energy, but the Enterprise had its dander up, now; the air so thick with malice it was barely possible to breathe.

"She's gonna blow!" Artie yelled, and I heard boots pounding on the floor behind me.

I reached to the Land, drew power into my bones, and Spoke with Words of fire.

"That's enough."

The dust devil congealed and fell to the floor with an audible thump.

The furniture froze in place.

The roaring stopped.

In the abrupt silence, one last piece of crockery fell off of a shelf and broke, quietly, on a musty hooked rug.

Beside me, Annora of Shadowood drew in a very, *very* long breath.

I could feel the weight of the Enterprise's attention, focused directly on me; and it wasn't the best feeling I'd had in my life. I felt the whole power of the Land singing in my blood, potent, alive, strong. I *was* Archers Beach, and my Word here was law.

"Release the virgins," I said. "Do it now."

The Enterprise hesitated. It . . . *growled*.

Oh, yeah?

"Are you," I asked, gently; there was no need, after all, to shout; "going to make me come down there?"

The growl . . . died. The kid from the Changing Land shouted and rushed forward, still holding onto the hands of the kids from Sempeki and Kashnerot. Behind them came the other three.

I swung back from the doorway, they jumped up the stairs, and I waved them on—

"Go! Outside! Annora!"

But Annora was already moving, sweeping them ahead of her, out of the Enterprise, into the dawnlight.

Me, I stood there a second longer, listening to the Enterprise brood.

"I'll come back," I said. "When I do, we'll talk about your role in the Age of Science."

The Enterprise . . . whimpered.

"It'll be fun," I told it, and turned on my heel and went away.

#

Annora was standing beneath the big tree at the edge of the Enterprise's dooryard, surrounded by the Midnight Vestals. Artie stood a little apart, hands twisting together.

"Kate." He started forward. I paused.

"How's the weather?" he asked me, jerking his head toward the Enterprise.

"Subdued. I'll be back to do some work. In the meantime, maybe you'd better clean up."

He grimaced.

"Some of that stuff was actual antiques," he said, half-accusing.

"So now the stuff that's left is worth more," I said, and moved on.

The Land showed me Artie standing behind me, indecisive for a moment. Then he squared his shoulders and walked into the Enterprise, closing the door behind him.

Annora had pulled her hood over her face. Right. It was dawn. Time for her to go.

Just one more thing, though.

"The Vestals of Midnight hold the Queen of Daknowyth's honor?" I said.

She bowed.

"For thirteen years, they do. At the end of their service, they are returned to their native Lands, provided with all and every comfort."

I turned to look at the kids; met the eyes of the Changing Land girl.

"You good with this?" I asked her.

"I'm good," she answered. And, like she felt maybe that was a little brief, added, "We'll have tutors. Three meals a day. Better'n what I got now. An' nobody'll touch us, on account we belong to the Queen."

"And by the time we are released to our own lives again," the boy from Cheobaug added, grimly, "no one will be *able* to touch us."

Kinless, Annora had said.

I nodded.

"Come see me," I said, to them all. "When your service is done."

"I'll do that, ma'am," said the girl from the Changing Land; the others murmuring their promises behind her.

The child from Sempeki stepped forward, bowing and offering the flower crown.

I bent my head gravely, and felt it settled gently on my hair.

The child stepped back, and I raised my head to look at the six of them, shining sweet and pure in the growing light.

"I regret that you were ever in danger on my Land," I said, which was nothing more than the plain truth. "And I salute your valor and your loyalty to each other."

I stepped back, and glanced at Annora.

"There's no Gate here, anymore."

"That is of no concern," she said calmly, "we ride upon the back of the winds."

Unexpectedly, she bowed, much lower than she needed to do.

"The Queen will be told of your service to Daknowyth, Kate Archer. You have also my thanks. Use my name as your own."

"Thank you," I said, with no intention of *ever* invoking *that* debt.

"Yes," she said, and opened her arms.

"To me," she said, and the kids moved in close, taking shelter in the expanding shadow of her cloak, until . . .

I stood alone in the dawn-light, the power of the Land singing in my blood.

Wolf in the Wind
Chapter One

Cael

"What took you so long? It coulda killed the whole town!"

Cael opened the door, and slid out of the truck. Oscar, in the passenger seat, watched attentively, mistrustful of the woman with her loud voice. He would have caught the smell of fear as clearly as Cael did.

The woman was blocking access to Storage Unit Number L9, holding a broom across her chest in a two-handed grip. Behind her, the roll-up door was rolled down.

"You didn't let it out, did you?" Cael asked, walking softly forward.

The woman wore an orange plastic jacket, with a picture of a *glashtyn* rising from the water. "Swamp Thing Storage" was stitched on the right breast; "Manager" on the left. Cael's own jacket carried the seal of the town of Archers Beach, "Animal Control" above it, and his name, "C. Wolfe," below.

"Didn't let what out?" the manager asked, frowning.

"The snake," Cael said. "It couldn't have killed anyone, if it was confined in the—unit."

"Wise ass," the woman snapped. "You dawdle your way down here, and now you're making jokes?"

It hadn't been a joke, but Cael had learned not to correct such statements, or to protest that he had been at another job when her call had come in, which he had been constrained to finish first. Fear made time run faster, and if, indeed, the captive was as dangerous as she represented, the manager had done well to keep it confined.

"Please stand aside," he said now, walking past, and bending down to grab the handle of the roll-up door. He didn't want her in the line of a rush, or a discharge.

"What?"

Fingers around the door handle, he turned his head to look up at her.

"Stand aside," he repeated. "You don't wish to be hurt."

"Right," she said, and hastily withdrew, stopping with her back against the animal control truck.

Cael nodded, spinning to the right as he threw the door up—and waited.

Nothing happened. There was no odor of brimstone, nor stink of poison. He sensed no enmity. Indeed, he sensed only the most minor tingle of life—slow, cool life.

"Kill it!" shouted the manager behind him. "What are you waiting for?"

Cael frowned. The interior of Unit L9 was crammed with large pieces of furniture, boxes were piled near the front, and a leather footstool had been placed atop the pile nearest the door.

On the footstool, curled in a puddle of late September sunlight that had found its way into the unit through the window in the roof—as a snake.

A very sleepy, contented snake.

"Kill it!" the manager snarled into his ear.

Cael turned to her.

"Why?" he asked, genuinely puzzled. "It's sleeping, and it is harmless."

"It's a snake!"

"Yes," Cael said patiently. "It is a snake. A northern water snake. It is harmless—no. It is better than harmless. It eats vermin. Its presence has been preventing mice from eating the boxes and fouling the furniture."

"A—look, you, I know a cottonmouth when I see one! They're mean-tempered and they're poisonous."

Cael frowned. He had studied hard to learn all the creatures of this Land that he served. There were, however, other Lands, and other creatures, of which he was ignorant.

He tipped his head, considering that last thought. While it was true that there were other Lands, snakes were much alike, wherever they were found. They did not travel far, save by accident, or the intent of those other than themselves. Unless this snake had arrived with the rest of the storage bay's furnishings, it was what it appeared to be—a northern water snake.

On the footstool, the snake moved, light glinting along its scales. Its head rose.

Cael reached for his link to this, his own, Land. Through it, he murmured to the snake.

"Tell me true: are you of this Land?"

"Yessss . . ." the snake answered, head moving slightly, its thoughts drugged with warmth.

"Lie easy," Cael cautioned it. "There is one here who calls your life forfeit; she believes you to be a poisoner."

There came an unsteady hiss, as if the snake was laughing, then it spoke, less drowsy now.

"That's not unjust; my mouth's a weapon, but my bite's for mice and vermin."

A pause.

"Though I'll make an exception, if my life's on the line."

"Yes," said Cael. "Lie easy and hide your teeth. I will need to move you, but I will preserve your life."

"'preciate it," said the snake, and lowered its head.

"Why haven't you killed it?" The manager's voice was shaking. "It's a cottonmouth."

"There are no cottonmouths here," Cael said, projecting absolute certainty.

He felt the manager's fear ease, somewhat. She went so far as to smile at him.

"Fine; it's not poisonous," she said agreeably. "Kill it anyway."

"No," Cael said, and held up a hand. "I will remove it. It is a useful creature in its proper place."

"Which ain't a storage bin!"

"Precisely. I will remove it to its proper place. Stand away."

"You ain't half a smart-mouth, are ya?"

"I lack the appropriate measuring stick," he told her. "Stand away; I will not have you harming this creature."

The manager stared, lips parted, face white with rage. She stepped forward, and he heard Oscar growl from the front seat of the truck. Cael made another small request from the Land.

The manager stopped, as if rooted, drew in a shaky breath, and used the broom to point at the drowsy reptile.

"Get that thing out of here," she said, voice raspy. "If you wanna take it home and keep it for a pet, that's all right by me. It's got no place in my storage park, understand me?"

"Yes," said Cael, patiently. "I understand. Please stand back. I will bring a container from the truck, and remove the snake."

She eyed him, and he clearly saw her desire to end the innocent life with her broom.

"Where you taking it?" she asked.

"To a safe place," Cael said evenly, and walked to the back of the truck.

#

The snake slithered out of the box at swamp side.

"Fare well," Cael told it. "Perhaps do not go into the storage units again. You might not be so lucky twice."

The snake paused, and lifted its head, cold eyes meeting Cael's gaze.

"There's some good eatin' over there," it commented.

"Is dinner worth your life?" Cael asked.

It moved its head, and the land brought Cael the impression of a sigh.

"Guess not." It paused. "You don't mind my askin', deah, what d'you happen to be, zackly?"

"I am an animal control officer."

The snake waited. Cael waited.

The snake turned and flowed across the mud, and down into a murky pool.

Cael sighed and got to his feet.

#

He pulled the truck into the garage, opened the door and slid out, clipboard in hand, Oscar behind him.

It took only a moment to open the back of the truck and make his inventory, then he locked up and headed for the office, Oscar at his knee.

"Good evening, John," he said, putting his clipboard on Karen's desk. He went to the time clock hanging on the wall, pulled his card out of its slot, slid it into the machine's maw.

KLUNG!

He removed the card, slotted it, then turned to face John, who oversaw his work here. John was not a bad man, by Cael's measuring. He had no personal tie to the Land, but that could be said of most of the people who lived within the boundaries of Archers Beach. Despite that deficiency, he had a genuine care for the creatures of the Land. John had once been what Cael was—an animal control officer—before his supervisor had stepped back from her duty, and John had been "kicked upstairs," as he said it.

That was the circumstance that had allowed Cael to take up the active care of the creatures of Archers Beach, while John sat inside at a desk, doing paperwork, negotiating with those above him in the town administration.

And taking complaints.

"Made yourself a lifelong friend with Jerri Evans over there at the storage factory," John said now.

Cael sighed, genuinely grieved.

"I am sorry that she called you," he said.

"Comes to that, so'm I," John said. He glanced down and held a hand out. Oscar being a gentleman who knew what rank required of him, he thrust his nose into John's palm, *hoofed* gently and wagged his tail.

John smiled slightly, some of the tension going out of his shoulders.

"Thanks, Oscar," he said, and looked back at Cael.

"You get that snake situated?"

"I returned it to the marsh," Cael said. "I—think it will not venture into the storage rooms again."

"Better not, if it values its life," John said. "Jerri Evans tells me she'll kill the next snake she sees on her property, don't care what kind, the only good snake being, according to her, a dead one."

"The snake today," Cael said. "It was not—any more dangerous than another snake. Not poisonous. Not a—cottonmouth." He looked to John.

"What *is* a cottonmouth?"

"A water snake, down Away. Sometimes you'll hear 'em called water moccasins. Sooner bite either of us than bother to swim away. Similar markin's to your northern water snake, which Jerri tells me you told her is what today's player was."

"Yes."

John looked thoughtful.

"Not that there's any snake that isn't dangerous, come down to facts. Filthy mouths. You get bit, the infection'll be enough to kill you if you don't get help quick."

"Yes," Cael said again.

"So that's me telling you to be careful around snakes," John said. Cael looked at him in surprise.

"Of course," he said. "A snake cannot go against its nature."

"Right you are, and you did right, moving today's back where it belonged. Now—" John sighed, and rubbed the back of his neck.

Cael waited. Oscar leaned against his knee.

"Jerri tells me you were too long answering the call, and gave her some attitude when you did get there."

Cael frowned.

John sighed.

"So, where were you before you went to see Jerri?"

Cael's face cleared.

"I was half-way up a tree."

John blinked.

"Pretty Boots got out again?"

Pretty Boots was not the true-name of the cat to whom Mrs. Angela Newton owed fealty, but that was to be expected; cats rarely shared their true-names. What was . . . distressing was that Pretty Boots made sport of her servant. Three times in the last two weeks, Cael had been called to bring Pretty Boots out of a tree. Today, he had remonstrated with her, trying to instill in her a sense of the obligations attached to her station.

Pretty Boots had tried to scratch him.

But none of this was John's concern.

"Pretty Boots did get out again," he said. "Mrs. Newton says that she unlatched the screen door with her paw."

"Don't doubt it; damn' cat's an escape artist." John shook his head. "'fraid we're gonna have to downgrade Mrs. Newton's calls to 'respond at leisure.'"

Cael blinked, thinking of the elder lady's face today when he returned the cat to her—pale and grateful to him for his service, her cheeks damp with tears.

"Mrs. Newton can scarcely climb the tree herself," he objected.

The Land brought him the taste of John's distress—and the metallic tang of determination.

"Nope, she can't. But she's taking up too much of a limited resource—that's your time—so she's gonna have to wait 'til after you shift snakes outta storage pods, and round up your various strays. You got nothing else on the list, then you see to Pretty Boots."

This, thought Cael, was not a practicable solution. There had been nothing else on the list when Mrs. Newton's call came in today.

He did not say this to John, however. Clearly, a solution had to be found for Pretty Boots, but that solving surely fell within Cael's honor as *trenvay*—a servant of the Land.

"Very well," he said.

John gave him a stare. John was a man of determination and courage, and the stare might have produced a tremor in the heart of a man.

But not in the heart of a wolf.

"Maybe you don't know who lives across from Mrs. Newton," John said, "so I'll tell you. Avis Marcant. You know, the councilor who wants you fired so her son-in-law can get put into your job?"

"Yes," Cael said, and did not add that the councilor also failed to approve of his appearance, and the place of his birth, as recorded on his birth certificate.

"There's a face says *Maine*," he had heard her say to her henchwoman, Bethany Miller, who had laughed lightly and answered, pretty voice full of malice, "Spends a lot of time out in the sun, don't he?"

He might have said to John that anything he did or did not do in order to please or placate Avis Marcant was doomed to fall short of hope—but he did not. John's position also depended on the whim of this petty lady. Cael owed nothing to her, but he did owe duty to John.

"I will remember," he said now, and Oscar thumped his tail on the floor, jaws parting in a particularly charming grin.

John's shoulders relaxed a little more, and he smiled, very slightly.

"Comedians," he said, and slid off the desk to his feet. "Go on along home, the both of you. You keep him outta trouble, Oscar."

The dog thumped his tail again. Cael smiled and turned toward the door.

Chapter Two

Kate

I never could figure out how I'd come to be on The Committee—that's the Fun Country Leaseback Committee to you. According to Jess Robard, I was on it because I was the owner-operator of one of the Named Rides, and therefore some kind of carny royalty. I didn't buy it, and said so, several times, loudly—but here I was, anyway—committee fodder.

God, I hate committees.

According to Jess, that was a feature.

"Kept everybody on point and focused, that's what," she'd told me, after the first meeting. "Service to the community, that's what you are, Kate Archer."

Yeah, some service. On the other hand, it wasn't like I was new to being of service to the community, being the Guardian of the Land known as Archers Beach. Not that the community, most of 'em, knew it—just those who happened to be tied to odd little bits of land, water, marsh; to this or that tree, or enterprise. The *trenvay*, those folks were called—minor magic users, and general Others. The rest of the community of Archers Beach—plain human folk—didn't much believe in magic, which was their protection, if not their guarantee of safety.

So, I'd gone to the meeting, and now I was walking back home from the library, where the body of the committee barely fit into the public meeting room, and pretty much overwhelmed the little window air conditioner.

It was warm for late September, clear blue skies and bright sun. The overnight would be crisp enough to require a sweatshirt or

31

long-sleeved sweater for an evening walk through town, and something a little more for the beach. The Atlantic Ocean was still warm, but the breeze was foretelling winter.

Despite the weather, there weren't many people in town. Fun Country had closed for the season, and Management, down in New Jersey, had refused to consider staying open 'til Columbus Day, even just on weekends. Which was completely in character for Management, and not one of owner-operators in the park ought to have been shocked, horrified, or pissed off by their decision, but—they were. At least, some of them were, myself not included. I hadn't thought it worth asking, truly, but the rest had been riding high on the victory of having bought the park and saved it from being condofied. Given that they'd already pulled off one miracle, why not shoot for two?

I hit the corner of Archer Avenue, waved to Lisa, who was serving up pizza slices to three teenage boys with skateboards under their arms, and turned right, toward the ocean.

There were maybe a dozen people in Fountain Circle, some occupying tables, some sitting on the wide stone edge of the fountain, chatting, or just taking in the day. Overhead, the flags fluttered noisily in the landside breeze.

To my right, there was Fun Country, gate locked; rides, games, and food counters all wrapped up and sealed for the winter. Just inside, to the left, the first ride everybody saw when they came through the open gate, was the Fantasy Menagerie Carousel, the oldest ride in the park, Kate Archer, owner-operator.

I walked up to the gate and wrapped my fingers around a warm metal bar, leaning in to look down Baxter Avenue. To my left, just behind the carousel, Summer's Wheel was naked metal spokes; the gondolas had been removed, wrapped in blue tarp, and lined up beneath. Down a little further, the Samurai was swathed in the same blue weatherproofing, the doors to the Oriental Fun House boarded up. The game kiosks down the center of the avenue were shuttered, just like the fortune-telling booth, the t-shirt shop, and Tony Lee's Chinese Food.

A breeze came up, smelling wistfully of egg rolls, and halfheartedly lifted a handful of dust into a swirl. The edge of the tarp covering the Samurai flapped in complaint, and the breeze died, leaving the dust scattered across the tarmac.

I sighed and turned away, my eyes going with a kind of involuntary dread to the commotion across the Circle.

In the recent past—by which I mean, the Season that had ended on Labor Day—there had been a midway across the Circle—games of skill and chance, a climbing wall, food vendors, henna artists, and all that sort of thing. It had been noisy, it had been crowded, it had made money for Management down in Jersey . . .

But not *enough* money.

Management had to protect its bottom line; that's what Management *does*, after all.

So, long story short, Management sold the midway to the highest bidder, which happened to be a new-made Boston-based LLC with condos in its eye, and it wasn't letting the smallest blade of grass get between its toes.

The midway had barely closed for the Season when the first crews arrived and began taking down the games, the booths, and the climbing wall. Two days after, the big equipment arrived on the backs of haulers, and they'd commenced in to digging.

Now, where the games and concessions had been, there was—a hole. Not much of a hole, yet, but at the rate the machines were working, it wouldn't be long before we were helping Chinamen climb up over the lip.

I shook my head, turned aside and went past the carousel, following the fence to the sidewalk's end, and on some more, over dry sand to wet, down to the very edge of the ocean.

I stood for a minute, looking out over the water. Tide was coming in; I took a deep breath, tasting brine, and sighed it out. To my left was the Pier. I could hear a sound check going on inside of Neptune's, at the very end of the boardwalk. Being a locally owned bar and dance club, Neptune's was taking advantage of every nice day and evening that September delivered, though it, too, would be closed by mid-October, when the tourists stopped coming in, and the townie traffic wasn't enough to keep the lights on.

Well. I smiled at the ocean, turned and walked under the Pier, along the water line, heading north, up the beach toward the old house on Dube Street, the waves crashing companionably on my right hand.

I emerged from the shadow of the Pier into the late afternoon sunshine, thinking about the hole in the ground where the midway used to be. Change . . . well, it *was* change. They don't call us the Changing Land for nothing. It's our greatest strength—and our greatest weakness.

Even though it was a necessary part of how the world operated—I didn't always care for change.

Up ahead, the waves charged the shore, foam flying like the manes of fey horses, each crash merging with the other, until there was one, continuous sound of the sea meeting the land, and—

A wave flew toward the shore, directly toward me, longer and taller than its comrades, striking with a boom that was all its own, engulfing me, then lifting me up, into arms that were solid, strong, and warm.

"Hey!" I shouted, part indignation, part laughter, and looked down into a big, brown face, black eyes bright as a moonlit night under black brows; broad nose, and a generous mouth, just now grinning in mischief.

"Hey, yourself," he answered. "Gotta be careful, walking the water's edge with the tide comin' in."

"Or else what?" I asked him, resting my hands on warm, broad shoulders.

"Else you'll get wet."

I was not, I noticed, wet. Nor was Borgan.

"I'm fairly warned," I said. "You gonna put me down or not?"

His face turned thoughtful.

"I could go either way," he said, "though I'm thinking you'll want to be set down."

The truth of the matter was that I wasn't all *that* eager to be set down. All things in their time, as they say, and given that, I hadn't given the man his proper welcome after our long separation of, oh—call it eight hours.

I bent my head to kiss him—one of my new favorite pastimes is kissing Borgan, right enough, but after that, it was bending *down* to kiss Borgan, which is only possible if I'm standing three steps up and he's on the sidewalk, or—

He was holding me against his shoulder, my feet 'way off the ground.

It was a thorough kiss, appropriate to the occasion of our reunion. It ended naturally; I sighed, and Borgan did, and I touched his cheek softly.

"Dinner and dancing at my place?" I asked.

"Sounds good," he answered, and bent to set me on my feet.

#

Cael was sitting on the front steps when we got to the house on Dube Street. He was barefoot, wearing a pair of khaki cargo shorts and a bright red shirt with a large gold foil design on the front, that might've equally been a flower or a bird. Oscar's head was on his knee, the dog's expression one of uncomplicated bliss, as Cael stroked his nose and head.

They both looked up as we approached, and Cael bowed his head, which I could *not* break him of, though he had finally managed to overcome his good up-bringing and—mostly—address me as "Kate," rather than "my lady."

By Cael's lights, Borgan was my consort, but not his lord, so the only thing he'd needed to be weaned from there was "sir."

"Good evening," he said now. "Kate. Borgan."

"Evening," I answered, and Borgan did, too, just like neither of us was concerned that Cael's presence would alter our pleasant evening plans.

Cael lived in the former rental unit at my back, just half-a-dozen steps from the bottom of the stairs. That particular arrangement was a compromise. I thought Cael and Oscar should have their own place, and Cael thought that his lady's Master of Hounds ought to be near to her hand, as she had no others to serve her. Not even pointing out that I had the entire Land of Archers Beach to serve me, not to mention the Lord of the Gulf of Maine holding an interest, had managed to shake him loose of the concept that no one could serve Lady Aeronymous—that being how I was styled in the land of my birth—more fitly than himself.

So, Cael lived in the studio, and had access to the house; and I lived in the house where I'd grown up, free to entertain my consort whenever and however I liked. Not that Cael was judgmental—he left that to Breccia.

"What can I do for you?" I asked now, because there was no use putting the thing off.

"I would like to speak to the Lady Breccia," Cael answered. "I hope that she will assist me in unknotting a vexatious difficulty with one of her own."

Breccia's own being feline. I shrugged.

"Sure," I said. "Come on up and we'll see if her ladyship's receiving."

#

Breccia liked Cael, despite the whole cat/dog thing, so it wasn't a big surprise to find her strolling across the kitchen toward us when we came through the door.

Cael glanced at Oscar, who recused himself, wandering over to the French doors overlooking the sparkling Atlantic Ocean, and sprawling in a splash of sun.

Cael dropped to one knee, and bowed his head, squinting his eyes in a cat smile.

"My lady," he said softly. "You honor me with your radiant presence."

Breccia continued forward, stropped herself along his knee, and sat facing him. She squinted her eyes.

"Everything that is gracious," Cael murmured.

Borgan at my back, I walked lightly around both of them and the kitchen table to reach the fridge.

"Ale?" I murmured.

"Sounds fine," he answered, and took the bottle I handed out to him. I got my own bottle, and leaned next to him against the kitchen counter, prepared to witness the negotiations.

"I bring news of one of my lady's kindred. It is not for me to judge such a one, but I feel that her behavior is . . . unworthy." Cael paused and shrugged lightly. "This may of course be because my understanding of things feline is . . . at fault."

Breccia squinted her eyes again, ceding the point and inviting him to go on.

"There is one who allows herself to be known as Pretty Boots. She maintains a modest establishment on Burdette Street, supported by an elderly and devoted servant. In former days, she would betimes leave the house to walk up and down the town. Since attaining a certain age and grace, she became less likely to exercise her rights in this way—until recently."

He paused, head bowed slightly, apparently awaiting whatever question Breccia might have.

I had a sip from my bottle. Borgan adjusted his lean against the counter so that his hip touched mine.

Breccia flicked an ear.

"Yes," Cael said. "Recently Pretty Boots has taken to letting herself out of the house and climbing the tree adjacent to her residence. Her servant has begged her to recall her station, to no avail. In my duty as Animal Control Officer, I have five times been called to physically extract her from the tree and return her to the care of her servant, who has been more distressed in each succeeding instance. Today, I took it upon myself to remonstrate with Pretty Boots, whereupon—she scratched me."

I sent a gentle query to the Land, which assured me that the scratch had been healed a bare moment after it had been received, which was no more than I had expected.

Breccia produced another ear-flick. Cael sighed.

"I am aware that it was unsubtle, but I am concerned for the servant, who is, as I have said, elderly, and daily made distraught by what seems to me, a most fallible wolf, her liege's willful neglect of her obligations."

He paused for a breath, and continued without waiting for a sign from Breccia.

"The situation has been made more desperate, as my supervisor today announced a new order to my duties: If I am called to succor Pretty Boots, I answer that call last. And, if the events of the day conspire so that I do not reach the last item before it is time for me to give over duty for the night, then I am to ignore the call entirely."

Breccia's tail snapped—to the right, to the left. And stopped, laid out on the floor behind her as straight as a ruler, and as stiff.

I drank off my ale and put the empty on the counter behind me.

Breccia still hadn't moved, and I was getting the idea that she wasn't half pissed off.

Cael must've thought so, too, because he dropped his head, keeping his eyes aimed at the floor.

"Lady Breccia, I am afraid for the old servant. Her heart may break beneath this show of contempt from one she has served so long. But more, I fear for Pretty Boots, that she has become lost to honor, and to all knowledge of her obligations."

Wow.

I realized I was holding my breath, and held it some more. Next to me, Borgan was doing the same.

Breccia looked like she was made out of the same rock as her chosen name.

Just when I felt like the choice was between breathing and fainting, Breccia stood. She stretched high, back humping, tail rising to describe a question mark. She strolled to the front door, and looked over her shoulder at Cael.

"Of course, my lady," Cael murmured, and came lightly to his feet. "Oscar will accompany us," he added, but Breccia had already turned her head away, such petty arrangements being beneath her.

"Why don't we all go?" said Borgan; his voice a rumble against my side. I turned my head around and looked up into his face.

"Sure," I said, "why not? It's a nice night for a walk."

Chapter Three

Kate

It *was* a nice night for a walk. I'd pulled on my denim jacket, and Borgan had rolled down his shirt sleeves. Cael hadn't bothered with long pants, jacket, or shoes. Breccia rode on his left shoulder, erect as a warrior princess in her chariot, and Oscar ambled along at his right knee.

"Best laid plans," I muttered to Borgan, who looked down with a half-smile on his face.

"Walk before's supposed to give you an appetite," he commented.

"That's *dinner*," I told him, sternly.

"Haven't had dinner yet, have we?"

I didn't dignify that with an answer, and anyway, here we were on Burdette Street, hard by a tidy little town cottage, in need of some cosmetics: a coat of paint, new shutters, maybe a new roof and she'd be good as could be.

There was a driveway on the right, mostly filled by an oldish Oldsmobile station wagon parked nose out. On the left of the house was a tiny square of land, entirely taken up by a large maple tree.

"Pretty Boots' tree?" I asked the night, and Cael nodded, as Breccia flowed down him like a jaguar down a cliff, and walked up the three wooden steps to the front door.

Oscar at heel, Cael followed her, and pressed the bell.

Borgan and I stayed behind on the sidewalk, and I felt the kiss of a briny breeze against my cheek, which was Borgan suggesting to anybody who happened to be watching that we weren't there.

A minute passed, dawdling. Then another. I felt Borgan shift beside me, like he was thinking about maybe stepping up and putting his hand on the knob—but just about then, the door *did* open and a tall spare lady with crystal white hair stood framed there, her attention fixed on Cael.

My attention was on Breccia, who casually strolled over the stoop and into the house like she owned the place. I might have twitched. Borgan put his arm around my waist, and I leaned into the solid warmth of him.

The lady hesitated a moment, glanced down, got a look at Oscar, and then looked back up.

"Why, Mr. Wolfe, what a surprise! Surely you don't work this late!"

"I am off-duty now," Cael told her. "I was thinking of you and of Pretty Boots and hoped that it would be all right if I came to ask after you."

"That's very kind. We're both fine. Just had our dinners and settling down to watch a little television, you know. Now that you're here, I have a chance to thank you for your patience and your skill in fetching Bootsy out of that tree. Honestly, I don't know what's gotten into her lately. Do you think I ought to take her to the vet?"

There was a little niggle in the back of my head, a suggestion that maybe I should look up, and over, where—

"Borgan," I said softly. "There's something *in* that tree."

"Any special kinda something?"

"It's . . . " I reached to the Land and asked a favor. Obligingly, it sharpened my vision, so that I could see into the branches, and the shadows near the bole, but by that time, I hardly needed the boost. Other senses were tingling, and I knew damn' well what it was.

"Willie wisp," I told Borgan.

There was a little silence, strongly seasoned with surprise. Up on the stoop, Cael and Mrs. Newton were running out of mutual admiration. She moved back a little, easing the door forward.

"Like to know what one of them's doing here," Borgan said finally, tipping his head back and staring up into the tree. "Being as the Wise cut us off."

"They say," I answered.

Cael gave Mrs. Newton a gallant little bow and a smile. He glanced down at Oscar, and the two of them turned.

Mrs. Newton smiled, nodded, and turned back into the house, the door swinging shut behind her.

Just before it closed, a white, orange and black streak flashed between door and jamb, flowed down the steps and was waiting on the sidewalk when Cael and Oscar reached it.

Cael nodded, and joined us at the end of the driveway, where he went down on one knee, offering his shoulder to Breccia, who hesitated, then leapt, landing lightly, and sticking her nose in his ear.

He rose, a frown between his brows.

"My lady Breccia would have us know that the house-tree harbors a—pest normally below the notice of Pretty Boots. However, this pest is of a kind that is particularly dangerous to her servant, therefore Pretty Boots at first tried to drive it away. When it ran, but returned, she changed her tactic, and now seeks to kill it. Today, it stung her. She was in pain from this wound when I took her off her branch. She tried to bear me with patience, but found me too much for her temper."

He paused, lips twitching.

"Pretty Boots offers an apology and hopes that my own wound does not hinder me in my duty."

"Well," I said. "Turns out Pretty Boots is right. There's a willie wisp in that tree—" I raised my arm to point—and lowered it.

"Which isn't there, now," I finished.

"Which matches up with young Bootsy's story," Borgan said. "It runs away, and comes back."

I saw a flicker of white out of the corner of my eye, which might've been Mrs. Newton looking out her window at Cael and Oscar standing at the end of her drive, a circumstance that might be worrying to an elderly lady living alone.

"Let's move on," I said, turning back the way we'd come. Cael, Breccia on his shoulder and Oscar at his knee, strolled with us.

"It is true that I have not detected any spoor," he said slowly. "And I swear to you, My Lady, I have been up that tree *many* times."

"Kate," I said absently. "I believe you."

Given that I *did* believe him, I, as the Archer of Archers Beach, or more specifically, the Guardian of the Land of Archers Beach, had a problem.

On the one hand, Pretty Boots had been right—willie wisps are vermin, powered by malice, and always hungry. While they aren't smart, they *are* cunning, especially in the matter of feeding themselves, and that was where this got to be my problem. As Guardian, it was my duty to protect the Land and those it nurtured. Angela Newton fell into that last category, and she was a willie wisp banquet.

See, willies . . . are from Away. '*way* Away. They're native to Sempeki, also known as the Land of the Flowers. What they eat there are the leftovers from spells and workings and the odd battle of wills—elemental fragments, call them. What they eat here in our very own Changing Land are—memories, the older, the better. A woman in her late sixties, early seventies, was likely to have a whole lot of memories.

"How'd it get here?" Borgan asked again.

"Maybe it got caught on the wrong side when the Gate closed," I said, sounding cranky to myself. "Who counts willie wisps to make sure none're missing?"

"Point."

"Regardless of *how* it is here, it is hunting," Cael said, practically. "It has seen a feast from which it must eat." He stopped, and looked over his shoulder in the direction of Mrs. Newton's house. "Pretty Boots is valiant, but valor alone is not enough for this. I will wait, and dispatch it when it returns."

"Might've gotten scared off by all the attention," Borgan said, but not like he believed it.

"Willie wisps aren't clever," I said. "If this one's been here since the Gate closed, it's hungry—well, they always are. But they don't have any natural predators here, and Mrs. Newton's got to be awfully tempting. I don't like her chances, even with Pretty Boots to guard her."

I looked at Breccia.

"How *is* Pretty Boots, by the way? A willie sting can go bad, if it's not cleaned."

The Land brought me an image of Breccia licking the swollen white paw of a pudgy gray short-hair, and a flutter along nerves that I knew well. The Land had helped Breccia heal Pretty Boots. I sighed in relief.

"Pretty soon you won't need me," I said, "and I'll retire to Florida." Breccia flicked her ears, and stared over my head.

"Right." I looked at Cael.

"Are you taking this on?" I asked him. "What about work tomorrow?"

"I will go to work tomorrow," he assured me. "The willie wisp will come again, tonight. It knows it wounded the house's protector, and in the dark it has an advantage."

I hesitated, but, hell, he was a grown man, and furthermore, he was familiar with the prey. In the Land of the Flowers, a child can dispatch a willie wisp with a single Word. It wasn't like Cael was going to be shooting a gun, unsheathing a knife, or even bringing his staff into play. One Word, and it would be over.

"Go for it," I told him, like he needed my permission. "What about Oscar?"

He tipped his head, considering.

"Borgan," he said gently. "Will you allow Lady Breccia to ride?"

"Sure thing," said Borgan, and put a hand on Cael's shoulder, so Breccia could walk across the bridge of his arm and settle on his shoulder.

Cael sank to one knee, and looked into Oscar's eyes.

"You will guard Kate this evening, while I track this quarry. The terrain is unfriendly to you, else you would be at my side, as always you are. Our reunion on the morrow will gladden us both."

Oscar didn't like it. He whined, and put his paw on Cael's thigh. In the end, though, he stood and came to my side.

"That's all right, then," I said, reaching down to fondle one floppy ear. "See you tomorrow, Cael."

"Yes," he said, and turned away, walking swiftly on bare, silent feet.

I turned to Borgan.

"Still up for dinner and dancing?"

He looked down at me, dark eyes beyond warm.

"Now, what happened to make you think I'd changed my mind?"

Chapter Four

Cael

Cael went up the tree lightly, first pulling the dusky air about him like a cloak. He found the branch from which he had liberated Pretty Boots that afternoon, noting the claw marks in the tender wood, then followed the trail higher into the canopy, until he found the nest.

In the Land of the Flowers, willie wisps nested on the ground, for the trees would not have them. This tree was not so nice, or perhaps it was only ignorant of the strange new bird.

The nest reeked of willie wisp and fouled *jikinap*, its shape a tangled oval of bright bits of trash.

Cael sat astride a nearby branch and looked about him. Despite the season, leaves were thick around the nest, though they were brown, rather than the autumn colors of red or orange. The branches directly below the nest showed welts where droppings had irritated sensitive bark. These things were expectable.

What was peculiar were the shreds of *jikinap* in and around the nest.

Willie wisps were not mortal creatures, like a hound or a cat or a wolf. They were creatures of energy, and they fed on energy. Particularly, they fed on *jikinap*—magical energy—by *absorbing* it. There should be no crumbs left over, to drip onto and scar the branch below it.

Unless somebody was feeding it. Seeding the nest with *jikinap* so that the willie was certain to return to this spot, adjacent to what ought to have been—save for Pretty Boots—easy prey.

Cael frowned.

What if, he thought, the willie wisp had not been here so long, after all? What if it had arrived in the Changing Land *after* the Gate had closed?

Foolish wolf, he told himself. If the willie wisp has arrived since the closing of the Gate, the question to ask was, who had carried it? It was possible to cross from World to World without using a Gate or a Door, but it was dangerous, even for *ozali*. To bring anything extra, especially something as unpredictable, improbable, and useless as a willie wisp, courted disaster. What could possibly be worth such a risk?

The leaves above him rustled in a sudden breeze, which brought him the distinctive odor of willie wisp. Cael took a breath, stilling even his thoughts, waiting with a predator's terrible patience.

The leaves rustled again, and here was his prey—large for a willie wisp, which lent credence to the theory that someone was feeding it.

The creature dropped into its nest, sparking bluely as it began to feed.

It was of some importance to choose the correct Word. Too potent, and it might fire the tree. Too meager and annihilation might not be instantaneous. There was no need to cause unnecessary pain. Even to a willie wisp.

The willie continued to feed, oblivious to Cael's presence. He took a deep silent breath, and felt the Word form in his mouth. It tasted of ice and lightning. It would do.

Cael Spoke.

The Word left a glaze of frost on his lips. It enveloped the willie wisp in a brilliant ball of snow, contracting—and melting away, leaving the willie yet in its nest, scarcely disturbed at its meal.

Cael stared.

The willie wisp burped violet sparks.

Well, then.

Already, a second Word was forming, but before it was whole, the willie started, as if it had understood its danger, and bolted downward through the leaves.

Cael lunged after it, all the way down to the ground. It was dark enough now to hide him from anyone looking out from their house. But wolves have excellent night sight, and he was able to see the willie wisp bounding across the street toward a house with one bright-lit window open.

The willie hurtled toward that small opening, Cael a bare two steps behind. He was across the street, across the sidewalk, and the Word that had taken form was too large and too dire for the hunting of vermin.

The willie wisp put on a burst of speed, the window clearly its goal. The Word in Cael's mouth bore his tongue down, scraped the inside of his mouth. He must Speak, or choke.

He Spoke. The Word left soot on his tongue.

Ahead of him, one bounce short of the window, the willie wisp exploded into thick ruby streamers—and was gone.

Cael stopped on the sparse lawn, shivering a little. He tested the air, which smelled of ozone, salt, leaf mold—but not of willie wisp.

Satisfied—relieved—he turned to go.

A circle of white-hot *jikinap* blazed up around him, arcing higher than his head, blocking out the stars.

Chapter Five

Kate

Dinner done, we carried coffee mugs out to the deck overlooking the sea. I'd grown up calling it the "summer parlor," and its season was just about past. I shivered, and leaned against Borgan's chest for more than just the pleasure it gave me.

Oscar followed us out and sat with his nose poking between the pickets. Not a happy dog, Oscar, but he was being polite about it. Truth told, I didn't blame him for being a little antsy. For all his talk of reunions on the morrow, I'd expected Cael home sooner rather than later, and it was getting along to being *much* later.

"Reckon the willie didn't come back?" asked Borgan, reading the room.

"Maybe," I said, feeling something like actual worry, now that we were talking about it. "Willie wisps aren't exactly rocket scientists. Could've seen something else shiny—and easier to steal—and gone off after that." I sighed sharply. "What I don't like is that it keeps coming back to that tree—to Mrs. Newton. That says there's a nest."

"Which means it'll come back," Borgan said. "Only maybe not soon."

"Cael's got work tomorrow."

Cael *had* to work tomorrow, or Councilwoman Marcant would be in the town manager's office *that* quick, demanding he be fired. Getting fired from a town job in a town as small as Archers Beach meant you weren't likely to get another job—at least 'til summer came 'round again and you could pick up something at Fun Country, making pizza, or drawing ice cream, any of which would be too much work for too little pay. Wouldn't make him any different than the rest of the townies; that's the way staying alive worked in a resort town. It was just the sheer—*malice* of the thing that got stuck in my chest. Cael was good at his job; his boss liked him; the town liked him, the critters liked him. But Avis Marcant *didn't* like him—and it had nothing to do with the quality of his work.

"Figure to take a walk back up the hill?" Borgan asked.

I sighed, and finished my coffee.

"Sometimes, it's hard to know the right thing to do," I complained, and felt his laugh in my bones.

"Now, I've never found that."

"Liar."

Another rumble of laughter.

There aren't any fixed hours that go with being Guardian of the Land. Or for the Guardian of the Gulf of Maine, either. The fact was that willie wisps *didn't belong* in Archers Beach. Willie wisps didn't belong *any*where in the Changing Land, but the whole of the Changing Land wasn't my problem. Thank God.

Cael was more than capable of taking care of a willie wisp, him being both my oathsworn, like they say in the Land of the Flowers, and through me, bound to the Land known as Archers Beach.

However, Cael had not yet taken care of the willie, and Cael had other duties to fulfill.

And, if there was one stray willie in town, who's to say there weren't more?

I sighed again and straightened away from Borgan.

"Looks like the willie wisp stops here," I said. "Coming?"

"Why not?" Borgan said, taking the mug out of my hand. "Being honest, I'd like to get a look at that nest."

"All right, then." I turned—

Oscar howled.

The Land shouted inside my head, showing me wet red streamers raining down onto a scruffy lawn, the blinding glare of a working snapping into being—and something that felt like nothing—like an absence—a *specific* absence of Cael.

Oscar howled again, long and desolate.

I spun, took a step through the doorway into the house—

And another step, out onto Burdette Street, at the end of Mrs. Newton's driveway.

Chapter Six

Cael

"You caught the *dogcatcher*?"

Cael froze. He knew that voice. Avis Marcant, the councilwoman John had warned him about. But she was a woman of the Changing Land, all but blind to *jikinap*, as well as the wonders and horrors it produced. She ought not to have been able to *see* a willie wisp, much less make a pet of it. As to these burning bars that penned him—

"I do not know what a dog-catcher is." That voice he did *not* know, and having heard it once, he discovered in himself a desire never to hear it again. "But I *do* know power, and this—entity—possesses a significant amount. It may be that it will do."

Oh, power, was that it? Cael sighed and allowed the power to flow out of him, through the bottoms of his bare feet, into the Land, where it would be kept for him. It was unusual for someone to set such a trap in the Changing Land, where *jikinap* so often malfunctioned, or changed into something else under the influence of the Land's special attributes.

In Sempeki, such hunts were common, the acquisition of *jikinap* being vital to survival. Sempeki was the homeland of his liege, and himself. But there was something . . . odd about the circle of power confining him.

It didn't *feel* like Sempeki.

Cael stood patient, which was not easy. The trap was not large, and the bars were hot. Now that he was empty of all power, they were also *interested*, as *jikinap* is always interested, in filling empty vessels with itself.

"If you want him, take him," said Avis Marcant. "He's nothing but trouble; whole town'll be better off if he's someplace else."

"What I want," said the other in their jagged stony voice, "is the key to this place. What I have caught is not the key. The question I now ask is: Is this creature—valuable?"

"Valuable?" Avis Marcant repeated. "He's worthless."

"In that case, I do not want it."

"I mean, not worthless!" Avis Marcant cried. "Not to *you*. He's worthless to this town, like the old woman across the street. And you still owe me."

Cael took a careful breath, tasting *jikinap*, and wished he could see through the blazing bars that confined him.

"Creature!" the other voice said sharply. "What is your name?"

Cael felt his lips pull back from his teeth in a snarl. Did she think him as untutored as that? And, yet, why *not* give her a name? It might play to his advantage.

"My name," he said, "is Abraham Lincoln."

"No!" Avis Marcant began. "That's—"

"Be silent!" the rocky voice grated.

A gasp, and a brief silence, before more hard words.

"Abraham Lincoln, be bound where you stand."

The flames died on an instant, and Cael considered his captors. He stared into Avis Marcant's face for a long moment before turning to the other, who was—not of Sempeki, nor yet of the Changing Land. The face was vulpine, dark; the craggy grey body wrapt loosely in a long white shift, the eyes glittering white as quartz.

He was, Cael realized, looking at one of the Wise—never a good idea, and especially now, when the Gate between the Worlds had been closed—by order of the Wise—so that the Changing Land might die, for the crime of having offended them.

Cael settled his feet firmly against the grass, felt the Land's readiness.

"Abraham Lincoln, how did you dispatch the willie wisp?"

Cael moved his shoulders. "I got lucky."

"Give yourself up to me." The Wise One leaned forward, eyes glittering; the grey hand stretched out to him veined with marble.

Cael dared not pulled the Land's power into him. He was its protector, through his oath to his lady, and his own inclination. If the Wise One touched him while he was connected to the Land, she would touch—she would *foul*—Archers Beach. That he would not allow. Better to stand here, empty of all power, and take his chances with her temper.

"He lied to you," Avis Marcant gasped, either released from the Wise One's will or stronger than he believed her to be. "His name is Cael Wolfe, and he's the worst dogcatcher this town has ever had."

It was not his true-name, the one that he had been born to, in Sempeki, but it was his name in this Land, that defined who and what he was, here.

The quartz eyes sparkled. Cael felt the draw of another power on his soul. There was nothing he could do to resist her, empty as he stood. So far as weapons went, he had only one that he might wield without calling on any power save that which resided in him alone.

He closed his eyes, and opened his secret heart.

Chapter Seven

Kate

The Land showed me what was going on across the street, and a friendly breeze brought me voices; the words as clear as if I was right there beside them. The fright in the rock suit was definitely one of the Wise; I could see the power blazing around her like a halo. Avis Marcant—why—or how—Avis Marcant was in this, I couldn't fathom, except for the part where she was trying to get the fright to take Cael out of Archers Beach. *That* wasn't going to happen.

What worried me—a lot—was this talk of a *key*. A key to *this place*. Was the place Archers Beach, in particular? Or the whole of the Changing Land? Either way, it made no sense. The Wise had cut us out of the natural orbit of the Six Worlds. They'd shut the World Gate, and were perfectly willing to let us die—it being not yet proved that we *would* die. I had the idea that what was going to die were the rest of the Six Worlds, but nobody'd asked my opinion, and anyway what could one Guardian of a swath of Land in Maine that was the sole support of a rundown resort town, do against the Council of the Wise?

"He's lying," Avis Marcant yelled, which got my attention, sure enough. I took a breath, reached for the Land—

And saw Cael shiver against the night air, falling to four good feet and leaping away as a large grey wolf.

Avis Marcant screamed. The Wise One shouted a Word potent enough to peel paint. Cael kept on going, making for the trees at the bottom of the street.

I reached to the Land, which ought not to have registered as power on the Wise's radar, but guess what?

Lightning stitched the night, heading right toward me. I jumped sideways, toward the house, hoping the incoming was just your casual killing blade of power, rather than something that had been personally addressed to me.

I was lucky. The bolt passed through the place I'd been standing—and hit the Oldsmobile with a crackle and a BOOM!

The door slammed open at my back.

"Get in here! Now!" Angela Newton shouted.

I didn't wait to be told twice.

* * *

Cael ran for the trees.

So far as he knew, they were *only* trees, nothing so terrible as the forest atop Heath Hill, the stronghold of his liege's grandmother and her consort. *Nothing* would get past *those* trees— possibly not Cael himself. The small grove he had chosen as his refuge in this moment of need would let him in, and—trees of the Land as they were, and owing fealty to Kate—they would protect him, man or wolf.

He loped across the asphalt. The undergrowth parted for him, and closed again as he slowed to a trot, stopping inside a small grassy clearing. Raising his nose, he tested the air, finding only the scents of an autumn wood. He heard no sound of pursuit, nor tasted *jikinap*. He might have had better information, if he touched the Land itself, but he felt himself safer as a simple wolf, innocent of power, fell or otherwise, and certainly innocent of the town's *dogcatcher*.

His hackles rose, and he felt a growl roughen his throat. Deliberately, he calmed his anger, stilled his thoughts. He was a wolf, simple and calm, hunting voles in the autumn forest, and nothing to draw the interest of one of the Great Wise Ones.

Around him, the trees waited. Cael shook his fur into order, and trotted across the clearing, disappearing between two pine trees, intent on finding the Heart of the wood.

* * *

The door slammed behind me, and I sagged against the wall. I was in a narrow vestibule, the wall across from me was papered with a seashell print that had probably been bright and cheery, once. To my right was the closed door. Across from me was a wooden umbrella stand with three umbrellas waiting to be of service, above it was a rustic wooden wall shelf, a set of keys hanging on one of the three iron hooks beneath a cheery stenciled Welcome Home!

To my left—was Angela Newton, standing in the doorway that must open into the rest of the house. She was wearing jeans and a sweatshirt, and clutching a pudgy grey-and-white cat to her chest.

"Are you all right?" she asked.

"I'm fine. I appreciate you letting me in. Things were getting a little hot out there."

"That woman!" Mrs. Newton exploded. "She's a menace, and her tame real estate agent, too! If she thinks I'm going to sell her this house—well, I *told* her I wouldn't! Why would I sell it? It's my home! My husband and I lived here all the years we were married, our kids grew up here—it's paid off! I grew up in this town! Where would I *go*, if I sold this house?"

"Won't take no for an answer?" I asked, easing away from the wall and sending a sharp glance at the door to be certain it was locked. It was, but there was only so much brass and wood could stand against, if Rocky the Wise decided she wanted in.

I extended a request to the Land, and felt living green energy wrap itself around the door frame, and weave across the door itself, which was something a little better in the way of protection.

"It's completely ridiculous! I told her no, that should've been the end of it! Then she produces this realtor, ready to write me a *blank check* and laughing at me when I said I wouldn't sell at any price. And now—loud music at all hours, fireworks after curfew—they're trying to force me out, I know that, and I know they'll find someway to make it worse, if I talk to the police, so I haven't, but if they're going to start threatening other people, to somehow make it my fault that these dreadful things are happening...."

Suddenly, she began to cry, her face turned away as if she was ashamed that I was seeing it.

I moved forward, and the cat in her arms—Pretty Boots, it must be—glared at me. I stopped, and the Land tugged on my sleeve. Not literally, but—just say the Land wanted my attention.

Ripples of power reached me—nothing at all like the usual feel of the Land, though there was something . . . tantalizingly familiar there. I queried, and got the Land's assurance that Avis and Rocky weren't on the lawn across the street anymore, which was only a limited comfort.

I asked about Cael, which was greeted with a sense of puzzlement before I got a glimpse of a big grey wolf moving quiet between trees. Nearby, that was the sense I got, and then the exact taste of the little spinney at the intersection of Burdette Street and Foote flooded my mouth.

All right, that was good. Wolf in the wood, no problem. Unless Rocky had gone after him, in which case I didn't like his chances. Not that Cael was without resources, but he wasn't drawing on the Land. I'd almost been killed by one of the Wise while I'd been standing in a power center in my own Land. I don't know what the Wise draw on, but there doesn't seem to be any limit to it.

The Land did the metaphysical equivalent of tugging on my sleeve again, and my senses were suddenly flooded with green determination, and a lingering taste of vanilla. The little wood on Foote Street, that was again, showing me its muscles.

"What should I do?" Mrs. Newton asked me, still clutching Pretty Boots to her chest.

I sighed and stepped toward her.

"First, you need to tell me who you are, and how long this Door's been here."

Chapter Eight

Cael

The Heart of the wood was a white oak tree. Cael the wolf paced toward it, drawn by the scent of vanilla and the cool sense of peace.

The tree stood on a knoll, uncrowded by lesser trees, strong pale branches arching out and up. Cael paused at the foot of the small rise, gazing up to leaves turned golden with September, light brown acorns clustered tight among them.

It was a worthy hiding place, and Cael doubted that either the Wise or Avis Marcant would seek him here.

Which only left the question of his next move. Kate would have heard the Wise One's assault and would have rushed to the defense of her Land. *That* was the cloth from which his lady was cut, and in his secret heart, he would have her no different. A wolf could love such a liege, even as he feared for her safety.

Nor was she without allies. Her consort, the sea lord, was not to be dismissed; nor those others who served the Land of which she was Guardian. All of those would have heard the racket of the Wise One's assault, and would be standing at the centers of their own small powers, ready to defend.

He ought to make his way to Kate's side, and assist in her defense of the Land. The only question remained was—ought he to go as wolf or man?

"*Another* one?" demanded a voice that was both pleasing and annoyed.

Cael lowered his gaze from the tree's proud branches, to find a sturdy figure clothed in a grey hoodie over a pair of grey sweatpants standing beside the ash-grey bole. The hood was thrust back, revealing short white hair, and a round, olive-toned face. Her eyebrows were umber, and her eyes a deep and glittering gold. She stood with her hands on her hips, and the sense that Cael caught from her was not . . . entirely . . . peaceful.

"I guess *you* got lost in the wind, too?"

Cael sat down and considered her. She stamped a bare foot against the knoll's short grass.

"Answer me! I, the White Lady of the Wood, command you!"

Disconnected from the Land as he was, still Cael felt the force of that command, as it flowed past him, the wolf disinterested in the lady's display of dominance.

She raised her eyebrows.

"This is a small holding," she said, her voice somewhat more moderate. "I already have one wolf to hold; I can't keep two. Go away. The wind has died; you can find your way home."

Another wolf? Who had been lost in the wind? The Wind Between the Worlds, would that be, that had been realigned as part of Prince Aesgyr's rebellion against the Wise? How long had this other wolf been here? Why? And did this have anything to do with the Wise One and the willie wisp?

These were, Cael thought, weighty questions for a wolf. He therefore opened his secret heart.

The White Lady glared at him.

"I said *go away*, not change forms."

"My apologies, Lady, but I belong to this Land."

Her glare softened momentarily, and Cael felt her query the Land. An affirmative was returned, somewhat aggrieved, which Cael also felt.

"You're not *trenvay*," she stated, which was both correct—and not correct.

"I am oathsworn to Kate Archer. I serve the Land through that bond."

"I can see you, and I can sense you, but the Land isn't nourishing you," she said, and tipped her head. "It's a little upset about that."

"I regret," Cael said. He could feel Land's distress, and longed to reach out to it, to find where was his liege and her condition.

"What are you doing in my wood?"

"Hiding, Lady."

Her eyebrows rose.

"Hiding from what?"

"Enemies of the Land, and of the Guardian."

She stiffened.

"You brought danger to my wood?"

"I think not, Lady. I withdrew myself from the Land, as you see, and assumed my other form, which is merely a part of my nature. Those enemies, they seek power; they follow power. As a wolf, and now as a man, I have no power."

"Fine. Go away. I don't want you here."

She was the goddess of the oak, protector of the grove, and surely she had every right to order him gone. Only, there was one other thing.

Cael rose, and bowed.

"May I," he murmured delicately, "speak with the wolf you hold here?"

* * *

"Door?" Angela Newton stared at me, shoulders tightening, her grip on Pretty Boots going even tighter. "The front door's been here as long as the house. As to who I am—I ought to be asking who *you* are!"

Fair enough.

"I'm Kate Archer. I own the carousel down in Fun Country."

Amazingly, she relaxed somewhat.

"I read about you in the paper," she said. "You made sure the park's going to stay in town."

That . . . was something of a stretch, but I wasn't going to argue about it this minute. Instead, I smiled and nodded, touched the Land, and extended a tiny curl of *jikinap*, seeking an answering flicker of power from Angela Newton.

There was no reaction, except a slight feeling of gentle care from the Land. Angela Newton was exactly as she presented—an old woman of mundane heritage, not a shred of other worlds or magic about her.

In the interest of completion, I examined Pretty Boots, who was, in her turn, just a cat, insofar as a cat can be "just."

"But—what door?" Angela Newton asked me.

The Door. Right. I'd felt it the instant I was inside the house, and the longer I stood here in the hall, the more uncomfortable I was getting. Private Doors between one or another of the Six Worlds shouldn't exist, according to the Wise, who liked to keep track of commerce between the Worlds, or maybe I mean smuggling. Despite that, such things *do* exist, but usually, they're warded and very quiet.

This Door was noisy, to the point that it was making my teeth itch.

"I'm thinking that I know what interest this real estate agent of Avis' has in your property," I told Angela Newton. "Mind if I take a look in your basement?"

She stared at me, then nodded. "All right. Is it something that can be removed? If I give it to them, will they *stop* and just—leave us alone?"

"It's a little technical," I told her. "I'll know more after I see how it's been installed."

Her forehead wrinkled a little at that, and her grip on Pretty Boots must have increased; the cat wriggled imperiously, and the woman bent to put her down.

Straightening, she waved a hand at me, turning toward the doorway behind her.

"Basement door's in the kitchen," she said. "I'll show you. And you'll want a flashlight."

* * *

Head on front paws, the wolf lay at the center of a fairy ring. Peaceful humors laced the breeze, and Cael caught the tang of forgetting, and something else, far more concerning.

He turned to the White Lady.

"Why did you imprison this wolf?"

She drew herself up, haughty goddess, and looked down her nose at him.

"She was wounded and confused when she came into my wood. I have the deer and the small lives to protect! I couldn't risk them, so I put her to heal."

That was very much the solution of a goddess, Cael thought. To heal the wounded—that would be at her core, as would the necessity to protect those who resided in her honor. To do both, while endangering neither would be a challenge, and the solution doomed to be uneven.

"Is she healed?" he asked.

The goddess looked troubled.

"In her body, yes. In her mind? I fear not. I note disturbing dreams and confusing thoughts. My best wisdom was to allow sleep to do its work."

"It is my intention to wake her," Cael said, "and to take her away from this wood." That would be true, even if the wolf were only a wolf, which, as he was becoming increasingly convinced, was not the case.

"You're worried," the White Lady said. "Have I done harm?"

It was never wise to criticize a goddess. Yet, what if another such fell to her hand? Her concern carried the scent of truth; she wished to learn better, and it was his to teach her.

"It's in my mind that this wolf is another such as myself," he said slowly. "Which is to say, she has two natures, and is not *only* a wolf. This duality of nature demands some care. If I am a man too long, I risk starving my wolf, and cutting myself off from the wisdoms inherent in that nature. If I am a wolf too long—"

"You may forget how to be a man," the White Lady interrupted. "In fact, I may have doomed her to a single nature." She turned to look at him. "How will I heal this?"

"First, allow me to wake and speak with her. It may be that not . . . much harm has been done. How long has she been here?"

The goddess blinked, and Cael bit his lip. What was time, after all, to a goddess?

"She came two days after Lammas," she said, surprisingly.

That . . . was not very long at all, then, Cael thought. Assuming that it had been Lammas just past that the goddess remembered.

"If that is so," he said carefully, "then she may well have escaped grievous harm," Cael said. "May I enter and speak with her?"

"Yes. Wake her and take her away. I give you leave."

She moved her hand, and the sweet humors of the air dissipated, even as the goddess herself faded away.

Cael turned to look at the wolf in the ring, who stretched, and yawned, and opened eyes as green as grass.

* * *

"Road's closed? What for?" asked the man in the red pickup truck.

Borgan gave him a friendly smile, and leaned close to the side window, shaking a little sea-calm off his fingertips.

"Got a little bit of a situation around Miz Marcant's house," he murmured, nice and easy. "Rescue and cops're on the way."

The sea-calm did its work, and the driver didn't say that the cops were less than five minutes away and the Rescue even closer, nor even ask was Miz Marcant all right. Instead, he nodded, and smiled at Oscar, sitting neatly at the curb.

"Right, then," he said, "I'll go 'round. Nice dog you got there."

"The best," Borgan said, stepping back, and giving a brisk wave. "Off you go, now."

Chapter Nine

Kate

It was a Door all right.

I could see the crisped, twisted remains of what must have once been significant wards, scattered across the stone floor.

Even standing back near the stairs, I could hear a hard wind howling—the Wind that Blew Between the Worlds, and nothing to play with, even on a good day. Every so often a gust would hit the Door and it would jump.

Not what you'd call a safe condition.

I would like it to be on record that I *did not* open the Door, just to see what was on the other side. I didn't even get close enough to put my hand against it, though I won't say I wasn't tempted.

There was no question in my mind that the Door was what Rocky was after, whether to ward it or open it was still an open question, though whichever it was, I was betting it wouldn't be good for this, my Land.

I looked around again at the burnt and busted wards, and winced. That had not been a trivial expenditure of *jikinap*. I didn't even want to think about how much power it was going to take to reweave and reinforce those so the Door was hidden again.

"One thing at a time, Kate," I muttered, and went back upstairs.

* * *

The wolf was almost dainty, brown coat shot with gold, ears well-set, tail held at neutral. Waiting.

Cael inclined his head.

69

"I am Cael, called the Wolf, oathsworn to Lady Aeronymous, who is also Kate Archer, Guardian of this Land. I bid you stand forth, and give an accounting."

The wolf blinked, lazily, and glanced over her shoulder at the ring and the wood beyond.

"The White Lady releases you," Cael said. "She has small lives, and gentle, to protect. Again, I bid you stand forth."

The moment stretched, even the wind was silent. If he asked a third time, she would be compelled, and he did not—

The air moved in a bright swirl and before him stood a woman of Sempeki, brown hair striped with gold and drawn back from a long-nosed face dominated by a pair of grass green eyes.

"I am Assa, called the Huntress. I am under geas to neutralize Corraiga the Wise, a known villain. I had tracked her to the threshold of the Changing Land before the Wind roared between the Worlds, and spun us apart. I was battered, burned, and, I fear, broken, before I found myself in the White Lady's grove, where I could scarcely recall my own name."

She lifted her chin and met his eyes firmly.

"I heard what you said to her, but truly, she has done more good than ill. I have lost the scent, though, and must begin again. I only hope that Corraiga has done no great mischief in the time since we were separated."

"I believe I know where this Wise One is," Cael said, and touched the Land, lightly.

An image appeared in the air before them, the white shift worn over the craggy body, the quartz-white eyes . . .

"Yes! That is Corraiga the Wise Where—"

At that moment, the Land screamed, the image of the Wise One replaced with another, more horrific, and the air was filled with ice.

Cael snatched Assa's hand and ran.

* * *

"Well, it was a good install, once upon a time," I told Angela Newton, as I put the flashlight back on the kitchen counter. "It's taken a beating, though. I can call in a technician, if you want; fix it up; so nobody knows it's there, like used to be."

"How do they—the realtor?—how does he know it's there now? Special instrumentation?"

I nodded. "Like that. I'm betting he was just looking to see what he could find, like those folks with their metal detectors, down on the beach—and yours just popped up, by chance."

She looked downtrodden.

"My bad luck."

"Not necessarily. Now you know it's got to be fixed. And I know how to get it fixed." Maybe.

"How much will that cost?" she asked, and it was on the edge of my tongue to tell her to wait until I'd found the right tech, when the house shook under the force of a blow from above. The Land showed me the roof, and a branch, and I didn't wait for anything else.

"The tree!" I yelled, grabbing the woman's arm and pulling her out of her chair. "Go, go! Out the back door!"

"Bootsy!" Angela Newton cried, twisting away from me with unexpected strength. She rushed down the hall. I jumped for the back door, wrenched it open—and here she came back again, at a dead run, the cat folded against her chest.

She flew down the back stairs, me right on her heels, hitting the ground, and hearing the Land wail just as I braked hard, staring into Avis Marcant's grim and determined face, over the barrel of a shotgun.

I reached for the Land. Avis Marcant yelled, which was reasonable, as she was suddenly knee-deep in dirt. Her finger tightened on the trigger—but the gun was no longer a gun; it was a piece of driftwood, still wet from the ocean.

Give her credit, she yelled again, and made a good-faith effort to bean me with it, only I ducked inside her swing, and she jerked back, the driftwood spinning out of her grip as she fell.

"You will give me the key!" Rocky snarled nearby, and I turned, seeing her approaching Mrs. Newton, *jikinap* crackling, one tendril whipping around to strike the woman on the shoulder.

She cried out in pain, and that right there was too much for Pretty Boots, who twisted out of her arms, and threw herself, claws out, at Rocky's face.

No question, it was a valiant effort, and Bootsy had a hero's heart—but the face was granite, the eyes were quartz, and Rocky was wroth. A swing, a connect, a sharp sound, like twigs snapping, and Bootsy was flying, then falling, limp as a broken flower, disappearing among the dropped leaves littering the grass.

Mrs. Newton screamed, and leapt forward, hands out, fingers curled—and was caught up by none other than Cael the Wolf, who spun away with her in his arms, while a woman I'd never seen before stepped closed to Rocky, seized her wrists and uttered a Word.

Time stopped.

When it started again, Rocky was immobile in the stranger's grip, her *jikinap* a whirling ball of vile and sullen lightnings, spinning and spitting above their heads.

I frowned. In the usual way of things, in a duel between users of *jikinap*, the loser's power was forfeit to the winner. Only, this winner didn't seem all that eager to claim her prize.

"Coward!" Rocky grated. "Are you afraid of power?"

"I am afraid of *your* power," the victor answered, and the Land showed me what she was spending to keep that loathsome ball at bay, even as she held Rocky in thrall.

"Assa, what would you?" Cael called.

"Give me a task to which I may release it! Quickly!"

I jumped to her side.

"Got just the thing!" I said, and met the bright green gaze she bent on me. "There's a Door that needs to be warded."

She gave me the grimmest smile I've ever seen on a woman's face, and the most satisfied one, too.

"Help me," she said.

"First thing is clean it," I said, reaching to the Land, which responded with surprising ferocity.

"Right," I said, and nodded at Assa.

"Give it to me," I said.

It was jagged, actively malevolent, and there was—so much. For a heartbeat, I questioned my plan, but it was already too late. Rocky's *jikinap* flowed through me, into the Land, and, following my thought, wrapped 'round the noisy door.

I staggered, and Assa caught me with a firm hand under my arm.

"Have to build real wards, later," I managed. "But that'll do for now."

I looked around.

"Where's Rocky?"

Assa's eyebrows twitched, and then she laughed, sweet as merrybells. "Rocky? I see. Her true name was Corraiga the Wise. She was unmade, of course, when you reft her of her power."

Of course, I thought, and couldn't quite find it in me to shed a tear.

Chapter Ten

Kate

It was done quick enough, after that.

Cael helped Mrs. Newton find where Bootsy had landed, and knelt with her while she cried. I felt the flicker, so faint, and Cael did, too. A second later, I felt the draw on the Land, then Mrs. Newton was crying aloud, "Bootsy! You're alive!"

Around about then, the cops showed up, and the Rescue; Borgan and Oscar, too. Borgan busied himself helping Avis Marcant get up onto her feet, and I felt a particular salty breeze pass by my ear.

Rescue gave all of us a rough-and-ready examination, and all of us, except Avis Marcant, refused transport to the hospital.

"It was Cael Wolfe who saved us!" I heard her say, as she was bundled up in a blanket and led to the ambulance.

"That's right, Avis," I heard the EMT answer, and recognized him for Jerry, one of the *trenvay* from the wetlands. "He's a good man, our Cael."

"None better," she said fervently. "And I'm going to tell the mayor so!"

I turned to look at Borgan about then, and Borgan looked at me, his face too innocent.

"What happens," I asked, "when she comes to herself?"

"Might not come back all the way," he said comfortably. "Little bit o'sea change never hurt nobody."

"Borgan—"

"So," Mrs. Newton interrupted, standing before us with Bootsy in her arms. "You'll be getting that tech for me, so this never happens again?"

I blinked, then, prompted by the Land, looked over to the side, where Cael and Assa Huntress were standing, heads together. I made a request, and heard her say, " . . . not back to Sempeki. I wish—an honorable service."

"Just a sec," I said to Mrs. Newton. "Comes to me that Assa used to do that kind of work."

I stepped over to the private conference.

"Excuse me," I said, "I couldn't help but overhear. Might be I could provide an honorable service."

Assa turned to me, green eyes wide.

"I am listening."

"Right. The elder and her cat are valiant and fierce in their protection of each other. But there are no servants, no children, no knights. And there is that Door in the basement, which is probably going to need a close eye kept on it for some time."

"You propose that I stay here to serve the elders, and to guard the Door."

"That's it. Unless that's not honorable enough for you."

"You will need to take an oath of fealty, to my lady, the Guardian of this Land," Cael said from beside her, and I saw Assa catch her breath as she realized what that would mean. That she would no longer be of Sempeki, but sworn and bound to the Changing Land.

The Land brought me the moment she made her decision, and an echo of the gladness that bloomed in her heart.

She dropped to one knee, and held out her hands, palms up. I put my hands over her.

"I, Assa, do swear that I will keep faith with the Guardian and the Land and never cause either harm. I will defend them and reverence them, and in all things obey them. This I swear upon my life."

The oath hit the Land with a *crack*! I felt power rise up, through me, through her, binding us, liege and oathsworn.

Assa gasped, and swayed on her knees. Cael stepped forward to catch her shoulders and help her stand.

"Done," he said, "and done well. Finish it, now."

"Yes," she said softly, and shook herself, flashing me a grin as she stood forward.

"Yes, Kate," she said, loud enough to be heard across the yard. "How good of you to remember! I still do that sort of work."

I brought her over for introductions, reaching down to the Land as I made them.

"Pleased to meet you," Mrs. Newton said, and Bootsy deigned to deliver a cat-smile.

"I am pleased to meet you, too, Grandmother," Assa said softly. "I will stay and be certain that you are left in peace."

"Course you will," Mrs. Newton said. "My own granddaughter? There's plenty room, and Bootsy will be glad of extra company." She paused and slanted a glance into Assa's face.

"Can you climb trees?"

"Grandmother," Assa said seriously, "I can."

"Good," said Mrs. Newton. "Then we're set. Come on in now, and I'll show you your room."

Assa followed her into the house, and I felt the ripple of the whisper she sent through the Land, for Cael's ears alone, and smiled.

Cael and Oscar left, heading for home; tomorrow was a work day, after all. Borgan and I walked out front to look at the damage that had been done by the falling tree.

"Looks like it's just that one branch come down," Borgan said. "She'll need a tree service, though."

"Or maybe not," I said, taking his hand, as we turned back down the street. "I'm thinking Assa has pertinent skills there, too."

He laughed quietly. "Might, at that."

Introduction to "Wolf in the Wind" partial

originally posted on Splinter Universe in August 2023

I started writing what was then called *Autumn at the Beach*, on—it says here—Sunday, May 10, 2020. In March of 2020, I'd had a mastectomy, and had started radiation therapy on May 7. I was worn out, scared, and restless.

So, I decided to write a book.

As a concept, this wasn't a bad one. It would give me something to focus my mind; it would keep me out of Steve's hair while he was writing the next Liaden book; and it would be—normal. Sitting in front of a computer for hours a day, typing, is what I *do*.

I chose to return to Archers Beach not only because the setting is comfortable, but also because—as I see in the clarity of hindsight—I wasn't in any shape to carry the complexity that is a Liaden novel, with all of its connections and history, in my head.

So, Archers Beach it was, and Cael the Wolf my chosen subject. Cael had only just gotten a job as the animal control officer at the end of the third published Archers Beach novel, *Carousel Seas*, and I was interested to see how that was going to play out.

My stance when working on a book is that the book comes first, and everything else is secondary. This has some limits, of course—bills still need to be paid on time; meals need to be eaten; dishes need to be done; radiation still needs to happen. But the Important Thing is the book. It takes center stage, and gives your brain something to chew on that isn't Just Worry. As it turned out, this was a very useful mindset.

Now, I wasn't writing very quickly, or anything like every day. But I was *writing*; I accumulated words, and eventually pages, so I could see forward motion.

Around the end of September, it was brought to my attention that we had a story commissioned for *Derelict*, an all-new short story collection from Zombies Need Brains. Since Steve was working on *Fair Trade*, it was my part—per our long-running arrangements—to write the story. I therefore put the novel aside to focus on it.

It was hard. I had no idea what I was doing. I flailed. I swore. I wrote a dozen starts, all wrong. And, finally, I wrote "Standing Orders," and sent it in, just making the December deadline.

When I next looked back in on *Autumn at the Beach*—I'd lost the thread, and the story Just. Sat. There. I did a little pushing and shoving, but it didn't so much as twitch an ear. So, I put it away, thinking it—or I—just needed a rest, and I'd come back to it.

. . . but I never did. January 15, 2021 was the last time I opened the file.

It now being August 15, 2023, the smart money says that I'm never going to finish writing the book now known as *Wolf in the Wind*; in fact, it is officially a Splinter.

Statistics: *Wolf in the Wind* is just about 10,500 words long—41 manuscript pages—in all its splintered glory. There are five chapters, which I'll be posting as I can do so, around doing other needful tasks, but no less frequently than once a week. We will be accepting donations, for those who are moved to hit the button at the bottom of each chapter. Eventually, all five chapters will be included in Splinter Universe Presents! uh, Volume Two, that will be.

And that's the story of the story.

Sharon Lee
August 15, 2023

Author's Notes

Doors Into Change

So, 'way back in 2006, I had some time on my hands. Steve was lead on the next Liaden book, and I'd always wanted to write a novel set in Old Orchard Beach, Maine, a place that I have loved long and without reservation. Also, the popular wisdom has always been that writers should have many irons—which is to say series placed with several publishers—in case Something Bad Happened.

I therefore took it upon myself to write a near-world, small-town fantasy novel set in Archers Beach, Maine. The book was titled *Carousel Tides*. When it was finished, late in the year, I sent it to our agent to shop around, which she did.

The novel was widely rejected throughout 2007 and 2008, before finding a home with Baen, in 2009, publishing in 2010.

You'll note I said above that I had wanted to write *a novel*, and that had been my intention. However, writer's brains are curious things; you never know what's going to take root in the dern things, and—long story short—my brain in produced two more novels following *Tides—Carousel Sun* and *Carousel Seas*, also published by Baen—and a half-dozen short stories.

For a long time, the brain seemed to be satisfied with this output in re Archers Beach, but then came a call from Michael A. Ventrella, who was putting together an anthology titled *Release the Virgins*. I agreed to write a story for it, as one does, and the writer brain obligingly forked over with "The Vestals of Midnight," set in one of the weirder corners of Archers Beach.

Then, in 2020, I began to write another Archers Beach novel, as detailed in the "Introduction" that proceeds this Note.

As stated in the "Introduction," I believed that "Wolf in the Wind," was doomed to remain a partial story, but my brain surprised me again. As long as I didn't insist on a novel, it whispered to me *just* as I was turning my attention to the next Liaden novel, it could provide an ending, and closure. Was I interested?

I was, of course, and the deal was struck. "Wolf in the Wind" was completed as a novelette, and appears in its wholeness in this chapbook.

This leaves "The Road to Pomona's," to account for, a story written in 1978, and rejected by The Earth until I stopped sending it out, sometime in the 90s, and eventually posted to Splinter Universe.

About then, Tom Easton sent a note saying that he was soliciting very short horror stories for a reprint-only collection called *Horror for the Throne*—did I have anything? I mentioned "Pomona." Tom asked to see it, and eventually acquired it.

"The Road to Pomona's" is not, strictly speaking, an "Archers Beach" story. It does, however, deal with some of the same ideas that powers the *Carousel* books, and I like to think of it as a precursor.

And here we are. If my life as a writer has taught me anything, it's to "Never say 'never.'"

So, I'll just say that . . . I can leave Archers Beach, the *trenvay*, the Guardian, and the whole of the Changing Land—I can leave them here, in relative ease and safety.

Thanks for reading.

Sharon Lee
Cat Farm and Confusion Factory
January 2024

About the Author

Maine author Sharon Lee is known for her SF and fantasy novels and stories, especially the Liaden Universe® series, which spans nearly thirty novels and many short works, transporting readers to a universe where diplomacy, trade, and traditions intertwine.

Her work is known for complex characters and intricate plotlines as she explores themes of loyalty, friendship, love, and the balance between tradition and progress.

Lee's passion for storytelling showed at an early age as she crafted imaginative tales for her own amusement. She met in a college writing course future writing partner, cat friend, and husband Steve Miller; they began collaborating in her universes shortly before joining households.

Sharon has also penned several solo novels, including the Barnburner mysteries and the urban fantasy Carousel Tides trilogy all set in her adopted state of Maine.

Lee's accolades include NESFA's Skylark Award and the Prism Award.

Sharon Lee lives in Maine with her husband-coauthor Steve Miller, and several very loud muses in the form of Maine Coon cats.

Novels by Sharon Lee & Steve Miller

The Liaden Universe®: Agent of Change * Conflict of Honors * Carpe Diem * Plan B * Local Custom * Scout's Progress * I Dare * Balance of Trade * Crystal Soldier * Crystal Dragon * Fledgling * Saltation * Mouse and Dragon * Ghost Ship * Dragon Ship * Necessity's Child * Trade Secret * Dragon in Exile * Alliance of Equals * The Gathering Edge * Neogenesis * Accepting the Lance * Trader's Leap * Fair Trade * Salvage Right * Ribbon Dance

   Omnibus Editions: The Dragon Variation * The Agent Gambit * Korval's Game * The Crystal Variation

   Story Collections: A Liaden Universe® Constellation: Volume 1 * A Liaden Universe Constellation®: Volume 2 * A Liaden Universe® Constellation: Volume 3 * A Liaden Universe® Constellation: Volume 4 * A Liaden Universe Constellation®: Volume 5

   The Fey Duology: Duainfey * Longeye

   Gem ser'Edreth: The Tomorrow Log

Novels by Sharon Lee

The Carousel Trilogy: Carousel Tides * Carousel Sun * Carousel
Seas
Jennifer Pierce Maine Mysteries: Barnburner * Gunshy

Pinbeam Books Publications

Sharon Lee and Steve Miller's indie publishing arm

Adventures in the Liaden Universe®: Two Tales of Korval * Fellow Travelers * Duty Bound * Certain Symmetry * Trading in Futures * Changeling * Loose Cannon * Shadows and Shades * Quiet Knives * With Stars Underfoot * Necessary Evils * Allies * Dragon Tide * Eidolon * Misfits * Halfling Moon *Skyblaze * Courier Run * Legacy Systems * Moon's Honor * Technical Details * Sleeping with the Enemy * Change Management * Due Diligence * Cultivar * Heirs to Trouble * Degrees of Separation * Fortune's Favor * Shout of Honor * The Gate that Locks the Tree * Ambient Conditions * Change State * Bad Actors * Bread Alone * From Every Storm

Splinter Universe Presents: Splinter Universe Presents: Volume One * The Wrong Lance

By Sharon Lee: Variations Three * Endeavors of Will * The Day they Brought the Bears to Belfast * Surfside * The Gift of Magic * Spell Bound * Writing Neep * Doors into Change

By Steve Miller: Chariot to the Stars * TimeRags II

By Sharon Lee and Steve Miller: Calamity's Child * The Cat's Job * Master Walk * Quiet Magic * The Naming of Kinzel * Reflections on Tinsori Light * Double Vision

Thank You

Thank you for your support of my work.

—Sharon Lee

Made in the USA
Las Vegas, NV
09 March 2024

86959660R00055